The White-Footed Mouse

story by Willem Lange

illustrated by Bert Dodson

www.bunkerhillpublishing.com
by Bunker Hill Publishing Inc.
285 River Road, Piermont
New Hampshire 03779, USA

10 9 8 7 6 5 4 3 2 1

Library of Congress Control Number: 2012937197

ISBN 9781593731090

Designed by Joe Lops
Printed in China

The
White-Footed
Mouse

I had the greatest dad that any kid has ever had.

When I was little, he took me for walks in the fields and the woods, and showed me how to find the nests of meadowlarks, and killdeers, and bobolinks.

On sunny days we played catch together for hours.

He taught me to swim and fish and paddle a canoe.

We built bluebird houses together and put them up on poles around our meadow.

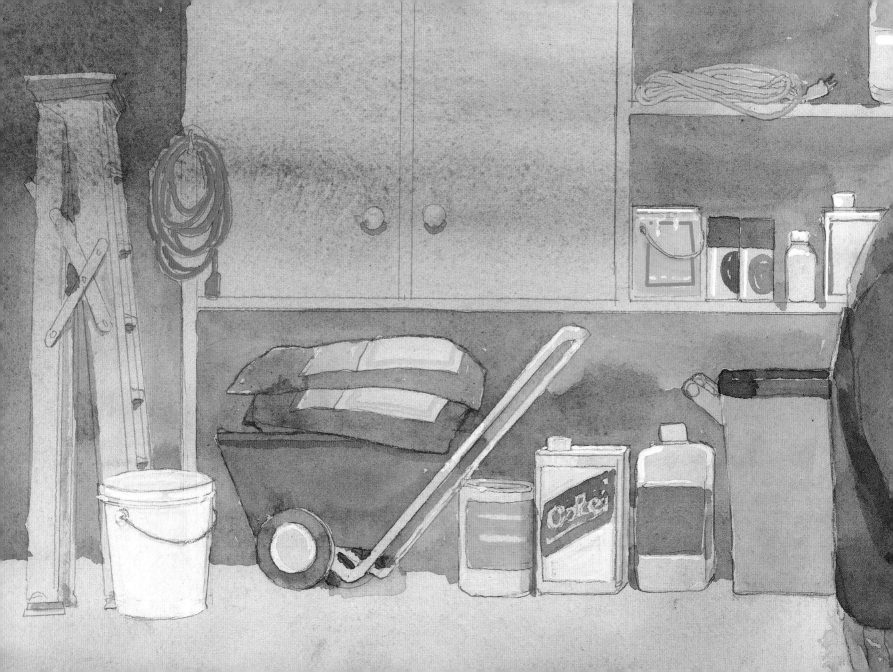

He taught me to shoot my little .22 rifle. Some day soon, he said, I'd be going with him to hunting camp, and I needed to know how to use it properly. I couldn't wait!

Dad was a really good hunter.

He used to say, "Don't ever point your gun at anything you don't intend to shoot, and don't ever kill anything – fish, bird, or animal – you don't intend to eat."

When I was eight, I was finally old enough to go. The first Friday in deer season I ran home after school and changed into warm clothes. Mom packed some groceries in my Dad's pack basket.

Dad came home from work about five o'clock.
We put everything into his old Jeep and headed up Hopkins Mountain toward our camp.
It was way after dark.

After a while we couldn't go any farther, so we left the Jeep and hiked up the trail with a flashlight. My pack was heavy. Dad took some of my stuff into his pack basket. It was really cold.

The snow crunched under our feet, and it seemed like a long time before
we saw the camp through the trees.

It was almost hidden in some hemlocks beside a little brook.
It was dark and spooky.

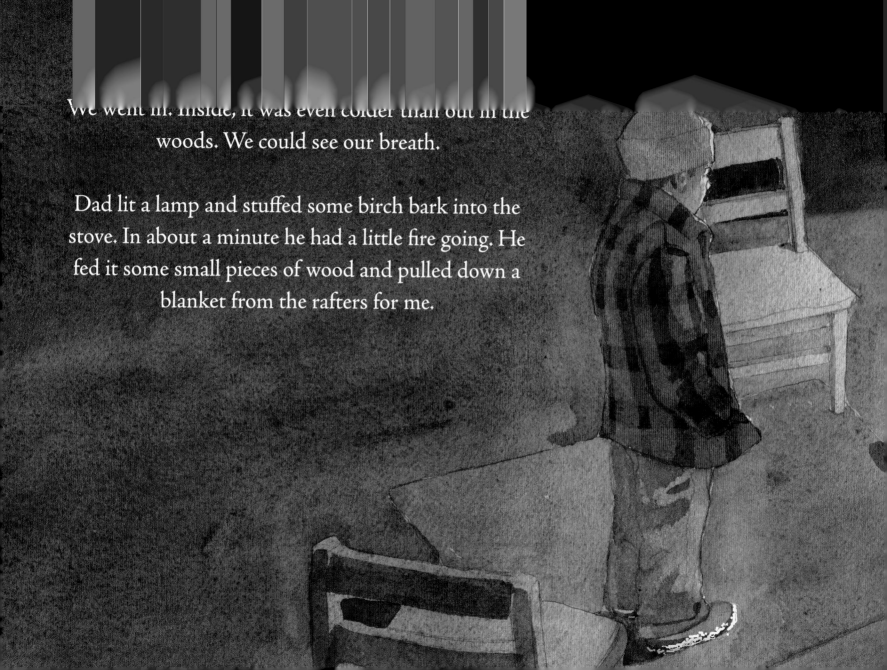

We went in. Inside, it was even colder than out in the woods. We could see our breath.

Dad lit a lamp and stuffed some birch bark into the stove. In about a minute he had a little fire going. He fed it some small pieces of wood and pulled down a blanket from the rafters for me.

We sat in front of the stove warming our hands
and eating cheese and crackers.

All of a sudden Dad said, "Look up! To your right!"

I looked. A little white-footed mouse was walking along the top
of the wall in the angle just below the roof.

He walked until he came to the spot right above where the stovepipe went through the wall.
Dad had insulated the pipe with a piece of clay tile packed with concrete.
It was always warm when the stove was going, but it never got hot.

The mouse slowly put one foot down onto the pipe to test it.
Then he climbed onto it and lay down, with his long tail curled over his nose.
He was watching us, but didn't seem to be afraid.

After a few minutes I got up and very carefully set a tiny piece
of cheese on the clay pipe right in front of his nose.

He sniffed at it, took
it in his tiny front
paws, and began
nibbling at it.

"Don't feed him," said Dad.
"I don't want mice in the camp.
I'll set a trap for him tomorrow."

The next day we hunted all day. We didn't see any deer, but sitting very still, we had a flock of chickadees all around us for a few minutes. And we saw a weasel, half-turned to white for the winter, peeking from a big hollow log.

In the afternoon we spotted a porcupine up a tree, chewing on the bark.
"Can I shoot him, Dad?" I asked.

"Yep," he said. "If you're sure you want to eat him." I didn't think I wanted to do that.
So we left the porky alone and walked away.

That evening in camp the mouse came back to the warm pipe. I got up to give him some more cheese, but Dad said, "Wait! Let me get the mouse trap. You can put the cheese on that."

"But, Dad! He's not bothering anybody! He just wants to get warm, like us."

"Doesn't matter. Mice in the camp, they've got to go."

"Well, okay," I said. "Are we going to have him for breakfast or lunch?"

We closed up camp and headed home Sunday afternoon. The mouse was back on the warm clay pipe, watching us. I know that mice probably can't wink, but I'm pretty sure that one winked at me.